Benjamin Bear

Says Thank You

CANDLE
BOOKS

Other titles in this series:
Benjamin Bear Says Sorry
Benjamin Bear Says Please

Benjamin Bear Says Thank You
Copyright © 2007 Lion Hudson plc/
Tim Dowley Associates

Published in 2007 by Candle Books
(a publishing imprint of Lion Hudson plc).

Distributed in the UK by Marston Book Services Ltd,
PO Box 269, Abingdon, Oxon OX14 4YN
Distributed in the USA by Kregel Publications,
Grand Rapids, Michigan 49501

Worldwide co-edition produced by Lion Hudson plc,
Mayfield House, 256 Banbury Road,
Oxford OX2 7DH England
Tel:+44 (0) 1865 302750   Fax: +44 (0) 1865 302757
email:coed@lionhudson.com   www.lionhudson.com

ISBN 978-1-85985-673-4 (UK)
ISBN 978-0-8254-7333-3 (USA)

Printed in China

Benjamin Bear

Says Thank You

Claire Freedman

Illustrated by Steve Smallman

The sun was up and shining.
Benjamin Bear was up too,
and feeling his happy bouncy self!

"Hooray!" Benjamin said, as he headed for the park. "There's nothing better than a day spent outdoors, playing with friends."

In the park, Benjamin's friend Lofty was playing football.

"Hello!" he called. "Fancy a game?"

Lofty passed the ball to Benjamin. THWACK! Benjamin kicked it SO hard, it flew across the field and landed in some thick bushes.

"Oh no," Benjamin cried. "I've lost your ball, Lofty!"

Just then their friend Fizzy waved to them from beyond the trees.

"I saw where your ball went, Benjamin," she called. "I'll fetch it!"

Moments later, Fizzy brought it over.

"Thank you," Lofty smiled at her.
But Benjamin didn't say thank you.
He was too busy practising his kicks.
Fizzy looked rather hurt.

"Benjamin," Lofty whispered to him. "Haven't you forgotten something?"

"What?" asked Benjamin in surprise.

"To say thank you to Fizzy for finding the ball. You don't want to upset her feelings."

"Oh no!" Benjamin gasped.

"Thank you, Fizzy," he said, giving her a big hug.

"That's okay, Benjamin," Fizzy laughed happily, hugging him back.

After playing football, Benjamin,
Lofty and Fizzy rushed off to the pond.
Stripe was there with a big bag of
bread, feeding the ducklings.

"That looks fun," cried Benjamin bouncily.
"Here," said Stripe, handing everyone some
bread. "Now you can feed the ducklings too."

"Thank you, Stripe," both Lofty and Fizzy said.

But not Benjamin. He was already throwing breadcrumbs.

"Benjamin," Fizzy nudged him. "I think you've forgotten something again."

"What's that?" Benjamin replied, feeling puzzled.

"To thank Stripe for sharing his bread with you," Lofty said. "He's looking rather unhappy."

"Oh dear!" Benjamin gasped. He didn't mean to upset his friend.

"Thank you, Stripe," he said.

"That's alright, Benjamin," Stripe said, looking cheerful again.

When the ducks had been fed, Fizzy and Benjamin decided to play on the swings.

But Flop-Ear and Hoppy had got there first.

"Would you two like a go?" they called kindly, jumping off.

"Thank you," Fizzy said. "We would."

"I love the swings," Benjamin cried, running over excitedly.

But then he stopped, and thought. He'd
forgotten something. Something *very* important!
Suddenly Benjamin remembered what it was!

"Thank you for giving us a turn on the swings," Benjamin said to Flop-Ear and Hoppy.

"You're welcome, Benjamin," his friends smiled.

Benjamin felt very pleased with himself as
he swung to and fro - and full of bounce!

And later, when Lofty treated everyone to ice creams, Benjamin was even happier.

"Thank you," he said. "I love ice cream."

"Yes, thank you, Lofty," the others added.

All except for Hoppy. Hoppy was too busy licking!

"Hoppy," Benjamin whispered in his ear. "Haven't you forgotten something?"

"What's that?" Hoppy said.

"To say thank you to Lofty for buying the ice creams."

"Oops, I forgot!" gasped Hoppy. "I hope I haven't upset his feelings. Thank you, Lofty," he said...

..."and thank you, Benjamin, for reminding me," Hoppy added. "It's only a little word..."
"But it means a lot!" Benjamin smiled.

Suddenly he felt so bouncy, he had to do a cartwheel –
which made all his friends laugh.

But best of all he felt bouncy on the *inside* – which
was his happiest feeling of all!

When someone is nice or kind,
It's good to say "thank you",
It shows that you appreciate,
The things they say and do!